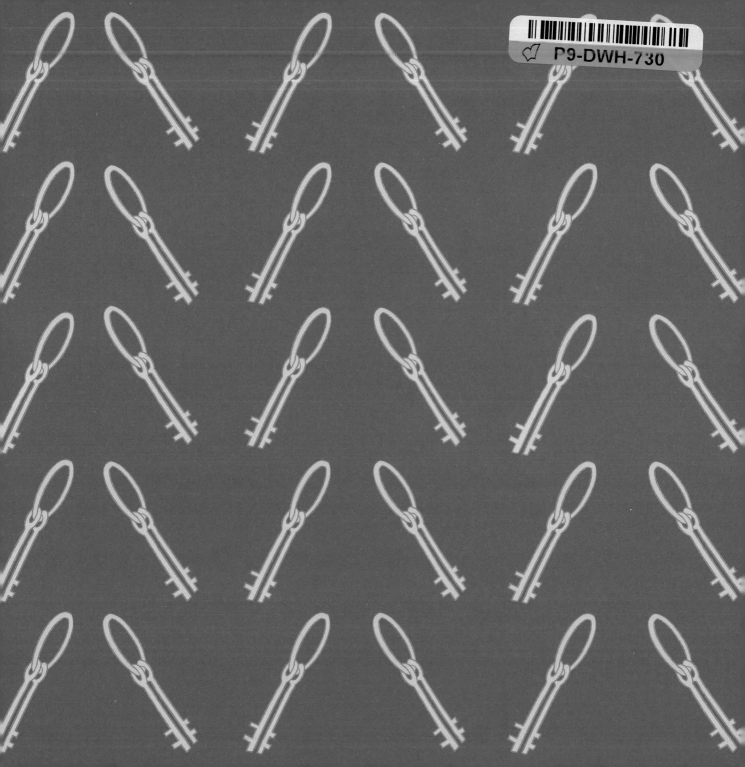

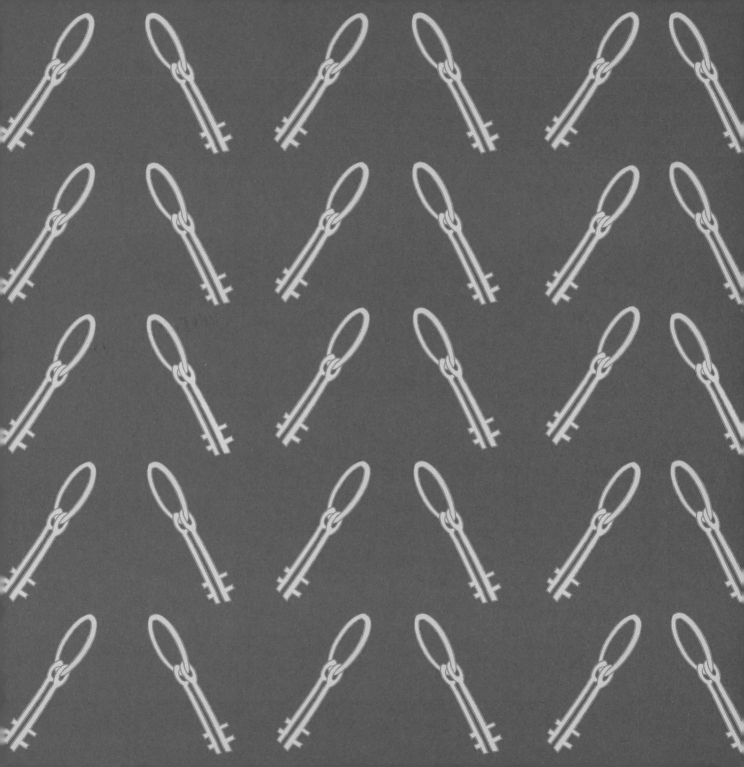

Curious George®

Good Night, Zoo

WITHDRAWN

Adaptation by Gina Gold
Based on the TV series teleplay written by Craig Miller

Houghton Mifflin Harcourt
Boston   New York

For information about permission to reproduce selections from this book, write to Permissions, Houghton Mifflin Harcourt Publishing Company, 3 Park Avenue, 19th Floor, New York, New York 10016.

ISBN: 978-1-328-97310-8 paper over board
ISBN: 978-1-328-97236-1 paperback

Cover art adaptation by Artful Doodlers Ltd.
hmhco.com
curiousgeorge.com
Printed in China
SCP 10 9 8 7 6 5 4 3 2 1
4500735036

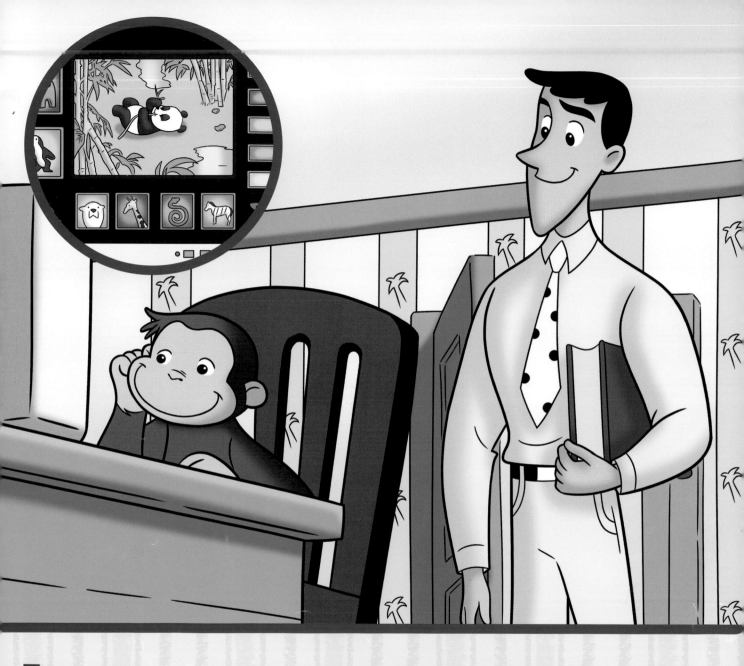

There was a new baby panda just born at the zoo. George had been watching the zoo's Panda-Cam all day. That panda was so cute!

"You know, the zoo's right down the block," the man with the yellow hat told George. "You can go see the panda for your—"
But before the man could finish, George was gone!

George got to the zoo and had one thing on his mind—baby panda, baby panda! But there were so many different paths at the zoo. How would he ever find the baby panda?

Then George saw a nice big map of the zoo. The baby panda's home was right in the middle of the zoo! The map helped him figure out which way to go.

Seeing the baby panda in person was much better than watching it on a screen! George could look at that panda for hours. And he did . . .

Before he knew it, it was dark. The panda was getting sleepy, and so was George. George knew he'd better get home. Time flies when you're watching a baby panda.

But when George walked out of the panda habitat, the lights were off. All the people were gone. Uh-oh. George was locked in the zoo! How would he find his way out?

George couldn't remember which path led back to the zoo's entrance. He started in one direction and spotted some keys inside a hut. Keys open doors, and doors let you out! All George had to do now was find the right door to get out of the zoo.

But there were lots of doors at the zoo.

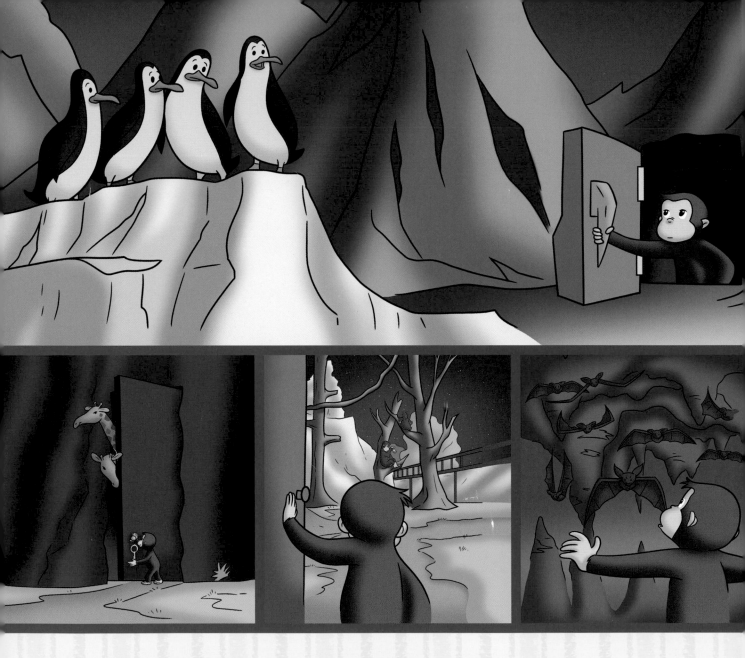

George tried door after door. None of them was the right one!

Soon, he was back where he started, by the baby panda. And so were the rest of the animals! George must have forgotten to lock all those doors he opened! What fun! George thought this was what all zoos should be like.

That is, until he realized that all the animals were waking the baby panda.

George knew what to do. He had to put all the animals back. He went as quickly as he could.

But none of the animals seemed happy. Maybe meerkats didn't live on ice. And those giraffes were awfully tall for that small cave. Were orangutans supposed to be in water? George knew that different animals had different needs. He realized he had put the animals back in all the wrong places!

George needed to get all the animals back to their correct habitats! The penguins lived on the ice, and the flamingos needed water. Luckily, George found an extra zoo map. Now he could easily see where all the animals lived.

Meanwhile, the man with the yellow hat was at home waiting for George. He sure had been gone a long time. The man looked at the Panda-Cam. George was still inside the zoo after closing time! The man rushed to go find him.

Back at the zoo, George had finally gotten the meerkats, orangutans, penguins, flamingos, bats, and giraffes back where they belonged. The animals were happy to be back in their own environments. Phew!

Yes, George had gotten everyone home . . . except himself! George checked his map. Luckily, he was very close to the zoo's entrance.

And even better, the man with the yellow hat was there waiting for him.
George climbed over the wall and jumped into the man's arms!

"Did you like the baby panda?" the man with the yellow hat asked. George sure did! He took the man's hand and they walked home together. George was exactly where he belonged.

Map It!

Did you see how George got lost when he didn't know which way the paths went in the zoo? Having a map sure helped! Here's how you can make your own map to help a friend or family member find something in your home.

You'll need . . .
- Paper
- A ruler
- Crayons or something else to draw with
- An object to find—like a ball or a shoe or anything that's bigger than your hand

What to do:
1. Walk around your home and make a list of all the rooms: the kitchen, bedroom(s), bathroom(s), and any other rooms you might have. Remember which room is next to which, then think about what that would look like from above.
2. Use the ruler to help you draw your map. You can use different colors for each room so they're easier to see on your map.
3. Put the object in the center of one room. Then mark your map with an X to show which room it's in.
4. Give your map to a friend or family member and see if they can find the object!

Mix and Match

George had trouble remembering which animal went in which habitat. Can you remember which animal went where? Think about the needs of each animal below and try to match them to their correct habitats.

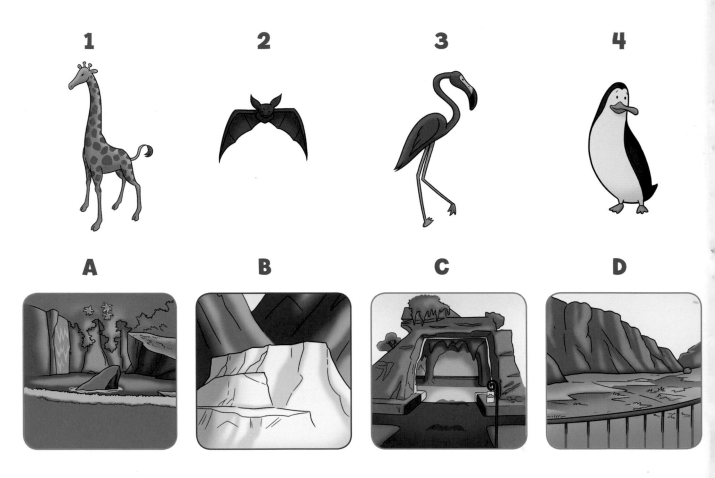

1

2

3

4

A

B

C

D